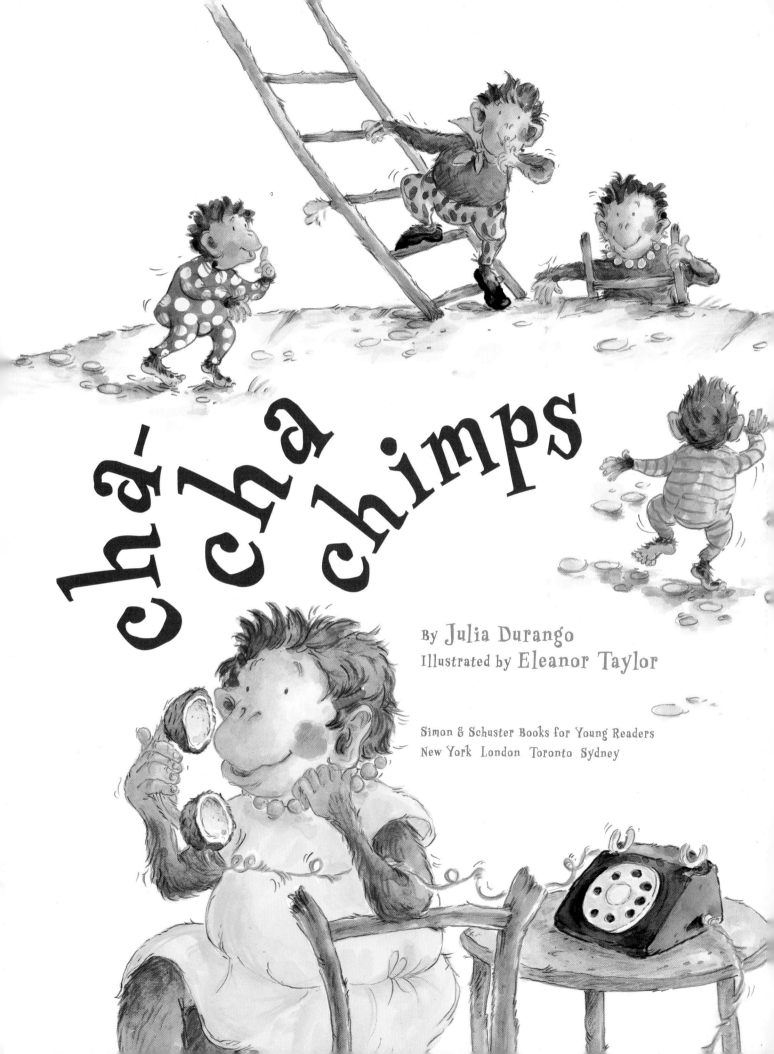

cha-cha chimps

By Julia Durango
Illustrated by Eleanor Taylor

Simon & Schuster Books for Young Readers
New York London Toronto Sydney

SIMON & SCHUSTER BOOKS FOR YOUNG READERS
An imprint of Simon & Schuster Children's Publishing Division
1230 Avenue of the Americas, New York, New York 10020
Text copyright © 2006 by Julia Durango
Illustrations copyright © 2006 by Eleanor Taylor
All rights reserved, including the right of
reproduction in whole or in part in any form.
SIMON & SCHUSTER BOOKS FOR YOUNG READERS is a
trademark of Simon & Schuster, Inc.
Book design by Einav Aviram
The text for this book is set in Blue Type.
The illustrations for this book are rendered in watercolor and pencil.
Manufactured in Mexico
10 9 8 7 6 5 4 3
CIP data for this book is available from the Library of Congress.
ISBN-13: 978-0-689-86456-8
ISBN-10: 0-689-86456-6

For Ryan, my cha-cha chiquitin, with love—J. D.

For Louis and Lola—E. T.

Deep in the forest in the dim moonlight,
ten little chimps sneak out for the night.

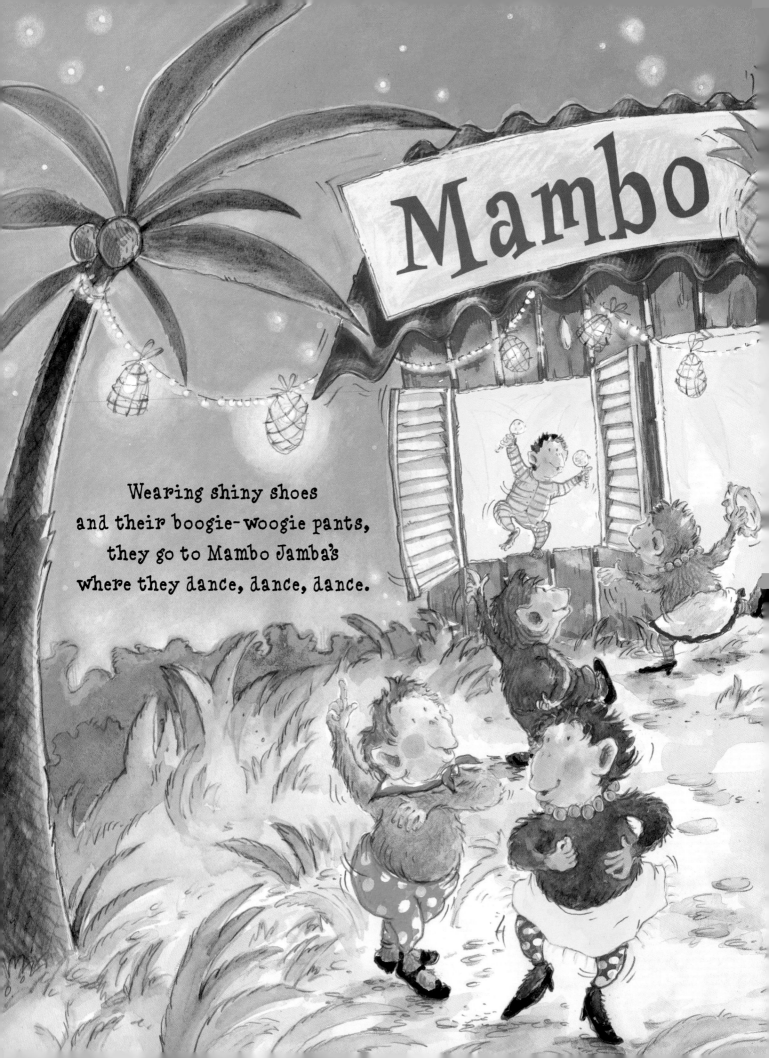

Wearing shiny shoes
and their boogie-woogie pants,
they go to Mambo Jamba's
where they dance, dance, dance.

Mambo

ee-ee-
oo-oo-
ah-ah-ah!
10 little chimps do the
cha-cha-cha.

Rhino hustles in
just to prove he's got the groove.
Shake it, Rhino! Shake it, boy!
Let's see that body move.

ee-ee-
oo-oo-
ah-ah-ah!
9 little chimps do the
cha-cha-cha.

Cobra slithers by,
and the crowd sways in a trance
'cause she likes to do the limbo,
but she *loves* to belly dance.

ee-ee-
oo-oo-
ah-ah-ah!
8 little chimps do the
cha-cha-cha.

Lion struts around
like the royal king of cool.
But five minutes later
he's a jitterbugging fool.

ee-ee-
oo-oo-
ah-ah-ah!
7 little chimps do the
cha-cha-cha.

Cheetah sambas in—*iay!*
She's looking mighty fine.
The chicos all go loco when
she starts a conga line.

ee-ee-
oo-oo-
ah-ah-ah!
6 little chimps do the
cha-cha-cha.

Hippo hams it up
as he tells the crowd a joke.
He makes them roar some more
when he starts to hokey-poke.

ee-ee-
oo-oo-
ah-ah-ah!
5 little chimps do the
cha-cha-cha.

Giraffe does the tango
with a rose between her teeth,
and gets into a tangle
with the dancers underneath.

ee-ee-
oo-oo-
ah-ah-ah!
4 little chimps do the
cha-cha-cha.

Meerkat macarenas
to a funky Latin beat.
His body shimmy-shimmies
from his whiskers to his feet.

ee-ee-
oo-oo-
ah-ah-ah!
3 little chimps do the
cha-cha-cha.

Zebra leads a jig
with her stripes all painted green.
The crowd gives a whistle
for the Irish clogging queen.

ee-ee-
oo-oo-
ah-ah-ah!
2 little chimps do the
cha-cha-cha.

Ostrich polkas round
like a wind-up whirligig.
He spills the cider barrel
so he stops to take a swig.

ee-ee-
oo-oo-
ah-ah-ah!

1 little chimp does the

cha-
cha-
cha.

Yikes! Mama Chimp comes
stomping through the door.
The band stops playing
as the dancers leave the floor.

The chimps try to hide,
and they skitter all about,
but when Mama yells . . .
ee-ee-oo-oo! . . .

the chimps come running out.

ee-ee-
oo-oo-
ah-ah-ah!
No little chimps do the cha-cha-cha.

Deep in the forest in the dim moonlight,
ten little chimps go home for the night.

They put their jammies on,
then they tumble into bed,
and wait for Mama Chimp
to kiss them each upon the head.

The chimps dream of dancing
under starry skies aglitter.
But one tiptoes out,
and she calls the babysitter.